Five Goodnight Kisses

Bill Hoffman

illustrated by Cheryl Casey

ISBN 10: 1542728487
ISBN 13: 978-1542728485

For Summer and Hunter.
Giving you Five Goodnight Kisses is
always a special part of my day.
- B.H.

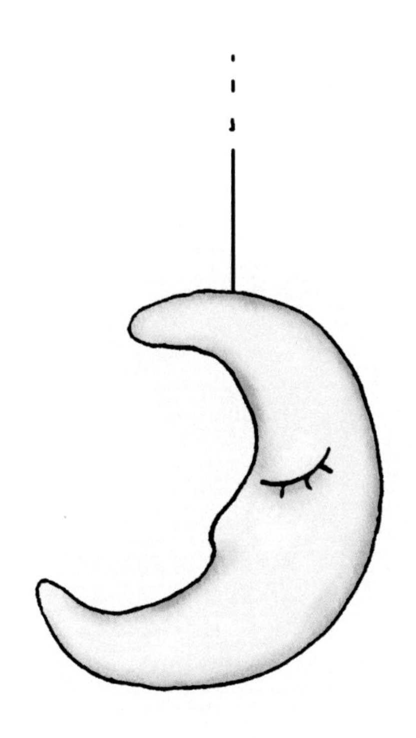

For my great-nieces and my one
outnumbered great-nephew, Kyri, Xyla,
Ariana, Arya, Kynleigh, and Gabrieal.
- C.C.

This Book Belongs To:

____

It was
time to go
to sleep for the
night and a little
girl named Summer
was trying her best
to stay up for just a
few more minutes.

Summer's daddy came up the stairs and she ran back into her room, jumping into her bed and pulling the covers up over her head.

"I know you are not sleeping," Daddy said out loud.

"I can't sleep yet, Daddy. I need my kisses," replied Summer from under her covers.

So her daddy kneeled down next to the bed and gave Summer a big ol' goodnight kiss.

"Good night my baby girl," he said.

"But wait, Daddy! You have to give me all five goodnight kisses," said Summer.

"All five?" her daddy asked.

"Yes, all five. You gave me the first one and the next one is an Eskimo kiss. They kiss with their noses 'cause it is so cold outside!"

The little girl then grabbed her daddy's head and rubbed her nose back and forth against his.

"Ear kisses are next, Daddy," Summer said. "This is how princesses kiss their guests at a royal ball. Remember, one kiss on each side."

Summer then placed each of her ears against her daddy's ears, which were much bigger than hers, and his scruffy face tickled her cheek.

"Okay then, good night now my sweetheart," Daddy said.

"Daddy, there is still one more kiss," Summer said smiling.

"Now we have to touch our foreheads together so we can look in each other's eyes once more before falling asleep."

"Alright now, good night my princess," Daddy said as he walked out of the room.

"Hold it right there, Daddy-o," demanded the little girl,

"I need to give my little brother Hunter his goodnight kisses!"

Daddy then picked Summer up and carried her into Hunter's room.

Summer leaned over and kissed her brother's little lips.

"Good night Hunter, my little buddy," she said while giving him an Eskimo kiss.

"I will love you forever, little buddy, 'cause you are so cute," Summer told her brother while giving him two big ear kisses.

"His face is not scruffy like yours, Daddy!" Summer said while giggling.

Next she placed her forehead against Hunter's and told him, "Sleep well baby boy, and have sweet dreams."

"Okay, my little love, good night," Daddy said as he tucked the little girl back into her own bed.

"But wait!" Summer said before her dad left the room.

"You already got five goodnight kisses and you gave five goodnight kisses to your brother. It is time for bed," Daddy explained.

"But wait!" the little girl said again.

"Yes, hunny, what is it now?" Daddy asked.

"I need five goodnight
kisses from Mommy!"

We hope you enjoyed this bedtime story. Now give everyone in your house five goodnight kisses.

About the Author

Bill Hoffman is an author who lives in Michigan. He has a wife, two children who love getting their Five Goodnight Kisses every night, and a dog who thinks she is a human. Bill and his family often go camping in the great outdoors. He spends a lot of time hiking but never gets on his treadmill. Turns out, treadmills are best for hanging clothes to dry. You can see his other books at WCHoffman.com

About the Illustrator

Cheryl Casey is an artist who lives in Texas with her husband and mostly-grown kids. She has a dog that looks like a bear, a fish that looks like a feather, and a cat that looks like a cat. Cats are resolute that way.
You can visit her website at cherylcaseyart.com

Made in the USA
Middletown, DE
10 February 2023